A KIDS LIFE

For Mom/Grams, for teaching us life lessons,
whether we wanted them or not.

A KIDS LIFE

Loving, Learning, Growing

ALANA KONIECZKA

ReadersMagnet, LLC

A Kids Life: Loving, Learning, Growing
Copyright © 2022 by Alana Konieczka . All rights reserved.

Published in the United States of America
ISBN Paperback: 978-1-956780-66-6
ISBN Hardback: 978-1-956780-67-3
ISBN eBook: 978-1-956780-65-9

All rights reserved. No part of this publication may be reproduced, stored in a retrieval system or transmitted in any way by any means, electronic, mechanical, photocopy, recording or otherwise without the prior permission of the author except as provided by USA copyright law.

The opinions expressed by the author are not necessarily those of ReadersMagnet, LLC.

ReadersMagnet, LLC
10620 Treena Street, Suite 230 | San Diego, California, 92131 USA
1.619.354.2643 | www.readersmagnet.com

Book design copyright © 2022 by ReadersMagnet, LLC. All rights reserved.
Cover design by Ericka Obando
Interior design by Mary Mae Romero
Illustrations Inspired by Michael Soucie

BEATING EVAN, THE BULLY AT HIS OWN GAME

EVAN WAS MUCH TALLER,
THAN OTHER KIDS HIS AGE,
AND IF ONE OF THEM BUMPED HIM,
HE'D GO INTO A RAGE.

IF HE WAS OUTSIDE,
SAW SOMEONE HE DIDN'T LIKE,
EVAN WOULD WALK UP TO THEM,
AND KNOCK THEM OFF THEIR BIKE.

HE'D PICK ON OTHERS IN HIS CLASS,
PROBABLY CALL THEM NAMES,
THEN HE'D GET REALLY MAD,
IF OTHERS DIDN'T DO THE SAME.

EVAN SURROUNDED HIMSELF,
WITH A MEAN LITTLE GROUP,
BUT ONLY SOME COULD JOIN,
HIS NASTY LITTLE TROOP.

IT DIDN'T TAKE LONG,
FOR ALL TO UNDERSTAND FULLY,
EVAN WAS TRULY,
A NUMBER ONE BULLY.

OTHER KIDS TRIED,
TO STAY OUT OF HIS WAY,
THEY DIDN'T WANT TO BE THE ONE,
HE PICKED ON THAT DAY.

BECAUSE EVAN WAS SO MUCH BIGGER,
AND HE WAS SO MEAN,
KIDS WERE AFRAID TO TELL ON HIM,
BECAUSE HE MIGHT CAUSE A SCENE.

BUT A GROUP FINALLY GOT TOGETHER,
AND HAD A SECRET PLAN,
THAT THEY WOULD STICK TOGETHER,
AND TAKE THE RIGHT STAND.

SO THE NEXT DAY WHEN EVAN,
STARTED HIS TROUBLE,
THE GROUP STUCK TOGETHER,
TO BURST EVAN'S BUBBLE.

THE GROUPS WERE UNEVEN,
SEVENTEEN AGAINST FOUR,
AND EVAN SOON LEARNED,
THEY COULD GET EVEN MORE.

THE GROUP FIGURED OUT,
IF THEY STOOD TOGETHER AS ONE,

EVAN COULDN'T PICK ON THEM ALL,
THE TROUBLE WOULD BE DONE.

EVAN TRIED A COUPLE TIMES,
TO SCARE THEM ONCE MORE,
BUT IN THE END,
EVEN HE KNEW THE SCORE.

BECAUSE THE ONLY WAY,
TO MAKE A BULLY STOP,
IS TO STAND ALL TOGETHER,
TO COME OUT ON TOP.

LIZ'S TROUBLES

IT WAS HARD FOR LIZ,
TO GO TO SCHOOL EACH DAY,
BECAUSE SHE LOOKED KIND OF DIFFERENT,
FROM THE OTHER KIDS AT PLAY.

ALL THEIR CLOTHES WERE NICER,
THAN THE ONES SHE HAD TO WEAR,
AND HER BACKPACK WAS SO OLD,
SOME KIDS WOULD STOP AND STARE.

WHEN HER FRIENDS WERE WALKING HOME,
THEY MIGHT STOP AND BUY A SNACK.
BUT LIZ COULDN'T AFFORD IT,
AND SOME WOULD LAUGH BEHIND HER BACK.

BUT THERE WAS SOMETHING,
THE OTHER KIDS DIDN'T KNOW,
LIZ'S MOM HAD LOST HER JOB,
BECAUSE BUSINESS WAS SLOW.

SO HER FAMILY WATCHED CLOSELY,
AT ANY MONEY SPENT,
LIZ COULDN'T HAVE NEW CLOTHES,
WHEN THEY HAD TO PAY THE RENT.

BUT ONE DAY LIZ DECIDED,
TO KEEP THE SECRET NO MORE,

AND SHE STOPPED HER FRIENDS,
WHEN THEY WERE WALKING IN THE STORE.

AS LIZ EXPLAINED,
WHY SHE DIDN'T HAVE EXTRA MONEY,
SOMETHING HAPPENED NEXT,
THAT WAS SORT OF FUNNY.

BECAUSE LIZ FOUND OUT,
OTHER KIDS HAVE PROBLEMS TOO,
THEY DIDN'T THINK ANY LESS OF HER,
FOR WHAT SHE WAS GOING THROUGH.

THERE WERE OTHERS WITHOUT MONEY,
SOME HAD A BAD GRADE,
OTHERS WERE IN TROUBLE,
FOR SOME BAD CHOICES THEY HAD MADE.

AND THEY ALL FELT BETTER,
ONCE THEY HAD THEIR HONEST TALK,
AND DECIDED TO DO SOMETHING,
AS THEY CONTINUED ON THEIR WALK.

WHEN THE GROUP WALKED IN,
TO SCHOOL THE NEXT DAY,
LIZ WENT UP TO THEIR TEACHER,
SHE HAD SOMETHING TO SAY.

THEY WANTED A PLACE,
WHERE ONLY KIDS COULD ALL MEET,
AND TALK ABOUT THINGS,
THAT THEY WOULDN'T REPEAT.

SEEMED MOST KIDS HAD STUFF,
THEY WOULDN'T TELL ADULTS,
BUT IF THEY TALKED ABOUT IT,
THEY SOMETIMES GOT RESULTS.

SO THAT'S WHAT THEY DID,
AND WHAT THEY STILL DO,
AND IF YOU TALK TO LIZ,
SHE'LL TELL YOU IT'S TRUE.

ELLAS GLASSES

ELLA COULDN'T SEE WELL,
SO SHE HAD TO WEAR THICK GLASSES,
AND SOME OF THE KIDS PICKED ON HER,
IN ALL OF HER CLASSES.

MOST OF THOSE MEAN NAMES,
MADE ELLA FEEL SAD,
AND HER FRIENDS DIDN'T LIKE IT,
WHEN OTHERS MADE HER FEEL BAD.

ELLA COULDN'T HELP,
THAT SHE COULDN'T SEE RIGHT,
AND THERE'S REALLY NOTHING WRONG,
WITH BEING SHORT ON SIGHT.

BECAUSE NO ONE IS PERFECT,
EVEN IF YOU CAN'T TELL,
AND SOME FOLKS GET SO PICKED ON,
THEY DRAW INTO A SHELL.

AND WE ALL NEED TO LEARN,
TO BE NICE TO EACH OTHER,
BECAUSE WE ALL HAVE FAULTS,
OF ONE KIND OR ANOTHER.

AND WHILE IT SURE MAY BE EASY,
TO LAUGH AT OTHER FOLKS,
ONE DAY IT WILL BE YOUR TURN,
TO BE THE SUBJECT OF THE JOKES.

BUT ELLA DECIDED,
NOT TO CALL NAMES BACK,
BECAUSE SHE KNEW WHAT IT FELT LIKE,
TO BE UNDER ATTACK.

SO ELLA ALWAYS,
WORE HER GLASSES PROUDLY,
TREATED OTHER PEOPLE KINDLY,
AND SMILED LOUDLY.

AND THAT MADE OTHERS LIKE HER,
AND WANT TO BE HER FRIEND,
BECAUSE OF THE POSITIVE,
MESSAGES SHE'D SEND.

SO IF SOMEONE IS DIFFERENT,
AND NOT LIKE YOU,
DON'T MAKE FUN OF THEM,
AND THEY WONT MAKE FUN OF YOU.

ELIZA'S NEW SCHOOL

ELIZA WORRIED ALL NIGHT,
ABOUT STARTING AT A NEW SCHOOL,
SHE KNEW SHE WAS AN AVERAGE GIRL,
WHO WOULD NEVER BE THOUGHT COOL.

SHE HARDLY ATE HER BREAKFAST,
TOOK A WHILE GETTING DRESSED,
IF SHE COULD WAIT ANOTHER DAY,
SHE THOUGHT THAT MIGHT BE BEST.

BUT ELIZA'S MOM KNEW THAT GAME,
PUT HER IN THE CAR ANYWAY,
AND SIGNED HER UP FOR SCHOOL,
SO SHE COULD START THAT DAY.

AND THEN ELIZA'S MOTHER LEFT,
AND SHE WAS ON HER OWN,
SHE THOUGHT THAT SHE'D NEVER,
FELT SO ALL ALONE.

ELIZA SAT IN THE OFFICE,
WAITING FOR AN AIDE,
THEY GAVE HER A LIST OF SUPPLIES,
THAT HER TEACHER HAD MADE.

THAT MADE ELIZA FEEL BETTER,
THEY WERE ALL SUPPLIES SHE KNEW,
AND SHE WAS PRETTY SURE,
THEY WERE IN HER BACKPACK, TOO.

WHEN THE TEACHER'S AIDE TOOK HER IN THE ROOM,
SHE SAW ALL THE STUDENTS STARE,
BUT SHE TRIED TO PRETEND,
SHE DIDN'T REALLY CARE.

ELIZA TOOK AN EMPTY DESK,
SAW THEY WERE DOING MATH,
SOMETHING SHE WAS GOOD AT,
SHE FELT ON THE RIGHT PATH.

AND THE VERY NEXT CLASS,
IT WAS TIME TO READ,
ELIZA GOT NERVOUS AGAIN,
TO JOIN THE STUDY GROUP SHE'D NEED.

SHE SAT IN THE GROUP,
POLITE AND NICE AND QUIET,

UNTIL ONE GIRL SMILED AT HER,
AND SAID THAT SHE SHOULD TRY IT.

SO ELIZA SMILED BACK,
AND READ HER PART,
THEN SHE KNEW,
SHE HAD MADE A GOOD START.

WHEN THE CLASS BELL RANG,
IT WAS TIME FOR LUNCH,
THE CLASS WALKED TO THE CAFETERIA,
IN A BIG BUNCH.

THE GROUP SAT TOGETHER,
AND TALKED AS KIDS WILL,
MAKING NEW FRIENDS,
GAVE ELIZA A THRILL.

ELIZA STARTED TO LEARN,
MOST SCHOOLS WERE THE SAME,
AND IT WORKED BEST,
TO TELL OTHERS YOUR NAME.

THE SCHOOL DAY WENT QUICKLY,
ELIZA MADE A FRIEND OR TWO,
JUST BY BEING HER FRIENDLY SELF,
WHICH WAS WHAT SHE LIKED TO DO.

WHEN HER MOM ASKED HER ABOUT SCHOOL,
ELIZA SAID "I HAD FUN,
I GUESS IT'S NOT SO BAD,
BEING THE NEW ONE."

ETHAN'S TEACHING

When Ethan came into class,
Everyone started to stare,
He was their first classmate,
In a wheelchair.

He was dressed like they were,
He had the same books,
But Ethan was aware,
He got some funny looks.

Ethan was used to the looks,
Inside it made him sad,
But he kept a smile on his face,
To keep from getting mad.

Just like all the others,
He tried to study and learn,
But when it came to gym class,
He never got a turn.

The other kids watched him,
As he wheeled down the hall,
Some would laugh at him,
Or block him into a wall.

And all that Ethan wanted,
Was to be treated just the same,

HE WAS WAITING FOR THE DAY,
THAT SOMEONE WOULD LEARN HIS NAME.

THEN ONE DAY AT LUNCH,
ETHAN SAT ALONE AGAIN,
THEN THREE GIRLS SAT DOWN WITH HIM,
AND GUESS WHAT HAPPENED THEN?

THEY STARTED TO EAT,
AND THEY BEGAN TO TALK,
ONE FINALLY GOT THE COURAGE,
TO ASK WHY HE COULDN'T WALK.

AND ETHAN TOLD THEM HOW,
HE HAD A BIRTH DEFECT,
AND IT WAS SOMETHING,
THE DOCTORS COULDN'T CORRECT.

BUT OTHER THAN THE WHEELCHAIR,
HE WAS JUST LIKE THEY WERE,
AND AS THEY SAT AND ATE THEIR LUNCH,
A GOOD THING STARTED TO OCCUR.

THEY STARTED TO BE FRIENDS,
AS THEY SAT THERE AND TALKED,
THEY WENT TOGETHER DOWN THE HALL,
ETHAN WHEELED WHILE THEY WALKED.

SOON THEIR OTHER CLASSMATES,
SAW THEY WERE HAVING FUN,
AND THEY WANTED TO KNOW ETHAN,
EACH AND EVERY ONE.

AND ETHAN LEARNED A LESSON,
THAT OTHER KIDS WEREN'T ALL MEAN,
MOST OF THEM WERE CURIOUS,
ABOUT THE FIRST WHEELCHAIR THEY'D SEEN.

AND THE OTHER KIDS LEARNED,
THAT DIFFERENT WAS ALL RIGHT,
WHILE SOMEONE MIGHT BE HANDICAPPED,
DIDN'T MEAN THEY HAD TO FIGHT.

SO WHEN YOU SEE SOMEBODY DIFFERENT,
PLEASE DON'T RUN AND HIDE,
IT'S NOT IMPORTANT WHAT THEY LOOK LIKE,
BUT WHAT THEY ARE INSIDE.

TOMMY'S LIBRARY DAY

IT WAS THE WEEKEND,
NO SCHOOL TODAY,
AND TOMMY WAS EXCITED,
IT WAS LIBRARY DAY.

TOMMY'S MOM TOOK HIM,
TO THE LIBRARY ONCE A WEEK,
LOTS OF PEOPLE WENT,
HE WASN'T UNIQUE.

TOMMY MIGHT CHECK OUT BOOKS,
MOVIE, DVD, OR GAME,
ALL THE KIDS AROUND HIM,
WERE DOING THE SAME.

TOMMY LIKED READING,
TAKING OUT A NEW BOOK,

MIGHT BE FOR THE SUBJECT,
OR THE WAY THE COVER LOOKED.

PLUS, THERE ARE OTHER THINGS,
THAN READING TO DO,
THE LIBRARY HAD PROGRAMS,
TOMMY LIKED THOSE, TOO.

THERE WERE PROGRAMS FOR ADULTS AND KIDS,
COOKING FOR A TEEN,
A COMPUTER CLASS FOR SENIORS,
AND EVERYTHING IN BETWEEN.

OR THEY'D GO OUTSIDE,
LEARN ABOUT FLOWERS AND TREES,
NOT EVERYONE LIKED THOSE,
ALLERGIES MADE THEM SNEEZE.

TOMMY ENJOYED HIS READING CLUB,
HIS SISTER, IRENE, DID TOO,
BUT THEIR BOOKS WERE DIFFERENT,
HERS WAS NANCY DREW.

THE LIBRARY WAS REALLY,
MORE FUN THAN SCHOOL,
TOMMY MIGHT LEARN,
IN A WAY THAT WAS COOL.

THE LIBRARY HAS,
SOMETHING FOR ALL,
A BOOK MIGHT BE BIG,
A NEW FACT MIGHT BE SMALL.

YOU CAN GO BY YOURSELF,
OR AS A FAMILY TOGETHER,
A GREAT PLACE TO GO,
WHEN THERE IS BAD WEATHER.

THE LIBRARY IS FUN,
WITH MUCH TO DO I HEAR,
AND IF YOU GO,
YOU MIGHT SEE TOMMY THERE.

VALUES IN RHYME

TO FIGHT,
ISN'T RIGHT,
BETTER TO TALK,
OR EVEN TO WALK.

TO CALL A MEAN NAME,
IS QUITE A SHAME,
TAKE SOME ADVICE,
TRY AND BE NICE.

NOT STUDYING IN SCHOOL,
REALLY AIN'T COOL,
BETTER TO TRY,
SO YOU CAN FLY HIGH.

IF YOU DON'T SHARE,
PEOPLE WILL STARE,
TRYING TO GIVE,
IS A NICER WAY TO LIVE.

IF YOU FEEL,
LIKE IT'S OKAY TO STEAL,
BELIEVE IT'S TRUE,
IT WILL HAPPEN TO YOU.

IF YOU THINK RULES,
ARE MADE FOR FOOLS.

I SUSPECT,
YOU WILL GET NO TRUE RESPECT.

IF YOU TRY YOUR BEST,
WHEN TAKING A TEST,
YOU MIGHT DO BETTER THAN THE REST.

TRY TO BE KIND,
AND YOU WILL FIND,
A PEACEFUL MIND.

IF YOU SMILE,
FOR A LITTLE WHILE,
IT BECOMES YOUR STYLE.

PUT THE VIDEO GAME AWAY,
GO OUT AND PLAY,
MIGHT BE A BETTER DAY.

IT'S OKAY TO PRAY,
DURING THE DAY,
IF THAT'S YOUR WAY.

IF EACH GIRL AND BOY,
CAN FIND TRUE JOY,
IT'S BETTER THAN A TOY.

IF YOU HAVE A GOOD HEART,
THAT'S A START,
TO SETTING YOURSELF APART.

IF YOU DO WHAT'S RIGHT,
YOUR SOUL JUST MIGHT,
SHINE WITH LIGHT.

MACKENZIE'S DILEMMA

Mackenzie had a problem,
Didn't know what she should do,
She had to face this problem,
It was a difficult one, too.

All her classmates were eating lunch,
But she forgot her favorite hat,
She quietly snuck down the hall,
And saw her good friend, Matt.

Matt was in their classroom,
Where he wasn't supposed to be,
Going through people's desks,
To see what he could steal for free.

MACKENZIE DIDN'T GO IN THE ROOM,
SHE SNUCK BACK DOWN TO LUNCH,
BUT THERE WAS TROUBLE COMING,
SHE HAD A FUNNY HUNCH.

WHEN THE CLASS CAME BACK,
IT DIDN'T TAKE VERY LONG,
FOR ALL THE STUDENTS TO NOTICE,
THERE WAS SOMETHING VERY WRONG.

SOME KIDS WERE MISSING MONEY,
ONE HAD LOST A BOOK,
AND MACKENZIE COULDN'T UNDERSTAND,
HOW INNOCENT MATT COULD LOOK.

AND MACKENZIE WASN'T SURE,
TO TELL THE TRUTH OR NOT,
SHE DIDN'T WANT HER FRIEND IN TROUBLE,
BUT WHAT WAS MISSING WAS A LOT.

SO SHE THOUGHT ABOUT IT HARD,
ABOUT WHAT WOULD BE FAIR,
AND THEN TRIED TO TALK TO MATT,
GIVE HIM A LITTLE SCARE.

SO SHE PASSED MATT A NOTE,
IT SAID I SAW WHAT YOU DID,
IF YOU DON'T SPEAK UP NOW,
I'LL TELL WHERE EVERYTHING IS HID.

WHEN HE READ THE NOTE,
AT FIRST MATT LOOKED MAD,

BUT AS HE THOUGHT ABOUT IT,
HE SOON LOOKED PRETTY SAD.

MACKENZIE THEN DECIDED,
BY THE END OF THE DAY,
SHE WOULD TELL ON MATT,
IT WAS THE ONLY WAY.

AND MACKENZIE TOLD THE TEACHER,
WHAT SHE HAD SEEN,
BUT IT DIDN'T MAKE HER HAPPY,
SHE FELT KINDA MEAN,

SHE KNEW IN HER HEART,
AS SHE WENT TO BED THAT NIGHT,
SHE HAD MADE THE PROPER CHOICE,
BY DOING WHAT WAS RIGHT.

AND HER CLASSMATES WERE HAPPY,
THE NEXT DAY IN SCHOOL,
THEY THOUGHT GETTING THEIR STUFF BACK,
WAS REALLY QUITE COOL.

AND THEY WERE PROUD OF MACKENZIE,
FOR WHAT SHE HAD DONE,
BECAUSE THEY KNEW TELLING THE TRUTH,
WASN'T ALWAYS FUN.

AND THERE WERE CONSEQUENCES,
FOR MATT TO PAY,
BUT THAT'S A STORY,
FOR A DIFFERENT DAY.

GRANDMA'S MAGIC PANTS

THERE ONCE WAS A GRANDMA,
WHO HAD MAGIC PANTS,
MONEY FELL OUT,
WHEN SHE STARTED TO DANCE.

SOMETIMES A LITTLE,
SOMETIMES A LOT,
HER GRANDCHILDREN WOULD,
PICK IT UP ON THE SPOT.

WHEN SHE WORE THOSE PANTS,
GOT UP FROM A CHAIR,
THEY MIGHT FIND,
CANDY SITTING THERE.

SHE LIKED TO SING WHEN SHE CLEANED,
OR MAYBE JUST HUM,
AND OUT WOULD DROP,
A WHOLE PACK OF GUM.

HER GRANDKIDS WERE HELPING,
HER WASH DOWN A WALL,
AND OUT BOUNCED,
A BRAND NEW SUPERBALL.

ONE DAY THEY WERE WALKING,
DOWN THE STREET,

A BOX OF CRAYONS,
LANDED AT HER FEET.

ON FRIDAYS THEY WAITED,
BECAUSE THEY KNEW SOON,
WHEN SHE TOOK A STEP,
THERE'D BE A WATER BALLOON.

SOME DAYS THEY LIKED,
TO GO FOR A WALK,
BEFORE THEY KNEW IT,
HERE CAME SIDEWALK CHALK.

WHILE NO ONE KNEW,
WHAT WOULD COME OUT,
THEY ALL SURE KNEW,
WHAT THE PANTS WERE ABOUT.

THE PANTS WERE THE PERFECT,
COLOR AND SIZE,
TO ALWAYS HIDE,
SOME KIND OF PRIZE.

WHERE SHE GOT HER PANTS,
GRANDMA WOULDN'T SAY,
BUT SHE ALWAYS WORE THEM,
ON GRANDCHILDREN DAY.

CONSEQUENCES

IF YOU TELL
A LIE,
IT WILL SHOW,
IN YOUR EYE.

IF YOU SAY,
WHATS TRUE,
PEOPLE WILL,
TRUST YOU.

IF THERE'S SOMETHING ELSE,
TO REMEMBER TO DO,
ALWAYS TREAT OTHERS,
LIKE THEY SHOULD TREAT YOU.

IF YOU RESPECT YOURSELF,
EVERY DAY,
YOU CAN HONOR YOURSELF,
IN EVERY WAY.

IF ANOTHER PERSON,
CALLS YOU A NAME,
DOESN'T MEAN YOU HAVE TO,
ACT THE SAME.

IF YOU HELP OTHER PEOPLE,
SOON YOU WILL SEE,

HOW NICE AND FRIENDLY,
THEY REALLY CAN BE.

IF YOU TAKE A PAGE,
OUT OF THE GOOD BOOK,
YOU WILL NEVER JUDGE OTHERS,
BY THE WAY THEY LOOK.

IF YOU'RE KIND TO OTHERS,
TREAT ANIMALS WELL,
THE WORLD WILL BE BETTER,
YOU WILL BE ABLE TO TELL.

IF YOU'RE NOT DOING RIGHT,
YOU NEED TO START,
AND SOON YOU WILL FEEL,
LOVE IN YOUR HEART.

CODY LEARNS GOOD LOSING

CODY WAS THE KIND OF BOY,
YOU THINK YOU'D LIKE TO BE,
HE KNEW HOW TO CATCH A FOOTBALL,
BEFORE HE EVEN TURNED THREE.

WHEN HE SHOT A BASKETBALL,
IT WENT RIGHT THROUGH THE HOOP,
AND HE COULD HIT THE FARTHEST,
AND SKATE A DOUBLE LOOP.

CODY WAS ALWAYS THE ONE,
TO WIN EVERY RACE,
WHEN THE STARTER SAID GO,
HE ALWAYS SET THE PACE.

BUT THERE WAS A BIG PROBLEM,
NO ONE WANTED TO ADMIT,
WHEN CODY WASN'T THE BEST,
HE THREW A BIG FIT.

LIKE THE TIME HE MADE THE THIRD OUT,
TURNED AROUND AND THREW HIS BAT,
HIS TEAM THEN HAD TO FORFEIT,
YOU CAN'T BEHAVE LIKE THAT.

THERE WAS A TIME HE PLAYED HOCKEY,
AND GOT KICKED OUT OF THE GAME,

HE HAD SO MANY PENALTIES,
IT REALLY WAS A SHAME.

SO EVEN THOUGH CODY WAS THE BEST,
ATHLETE IN THE WHOLE TOWN,
WHEN IT WAS TIME TO PICK TEAMS,
NO ONE WANTED HIM AROUND.

AND CODY STARTED TO GET LONELY,
HE FELT KIND OF SAD,
AND KNEW THERE WAS ONLY ONE WAY,
TO GET OVER FEELING BAD.

HE WENT TO THE PARK,
AND ASKED IF HE COULD PLAY,
BUT FIRST HE HAD TO LISTEN,
TO WHAT OTHERS HAD TO SAY.

THEY TOLD HIM HE COULD PLAY,
IF HE COULD LEARN HOW TO LOSE,
TO PLAY IN THIS GAME,
HE WAS GOING TO HAVE TO CHOOSE.

CODY COULD TRY HARD BUT HAVE FUN,
HE HAD TO BE A GOOD SPORT,
BE A GOOD TEAMMATE,
ON AND OFF THE COURT.

CODY THOUGHT FOR A WHILE,
AND FINALLY UNDERSTOOD,
THERE WAS MORE TO WINNING,
THAN JUST BEING GOOD.

IT'S ABOUT WORKING TOGETHER,
TO TRY AND WIN A GAME,
BECAUSE EACH PERSON'S ABILITY,
MAY NOT BE THE SAME.

AND CODY KNEW HE WOULD ALWAYS,
REMEMBER THE DAY,
HE LEARNED A VALUABLE LESSON,
ON HOW TO REALLY PLAY.

Michael Learns About Sportsmanship

Michael was the kind of boy, some kids thought was cool,

HE WAS ONE OF THE BEST ATHLETES,
IN THE WHOLE ENTIRE SCHOOL.

A REALLY FAST RUNNER,
HE SURE COULD HIT A BALL,
NEVER MISSED A BASKET,
OR LET THE FOOTBALL FALL.

OUTSIDE AT LUNCH,
OR IN GYM CLASS,
CAPTAINS PICKED HIM FIRST,
THEY KNEW HE'D CATCH THE PASS.

BUT THERE WAS A BIG PROBLEM,
WHEN MICHAEL PLAYED A GAME,
SOMETIMES HIS TEAM LOST,
NOT ALL PEOPLE PLAY THE SAME.

AND EVERYONE WOULD KNOW,
THAT MICHAEL WAS MAD,
SOME OF WHAT HE DID AND SAID,
MADE OTHER PLAYERS SAD.

HE MIGHT CALL THEM A NAME,
OR THROW HIS BAT,
ONCE I EVEN HEARD,
HE RIPPED A TEAMMATE'S HAT.

ALL THE PLAYERS AGREED,
GOOD PLAYER BUT POOR SPORT,
QUIT PICKING HIM FOR BASEBALL,
DON'T LET HIM ON THE COURT.

BUT MICHAEL GOT LUCKY,
HE HAD AN OLDER BROTHER,
WHO COULD TEACH HIM HOW,
TO TREAT ONE ANOTHER.

HIS BROTHER SAT HIM DOWN,
SO THEY COULD CONVERSATE,
AND MICHAEL LEARNED SOME LESSONS,
BEFORE IT WAS TOO LATE.

"SOME KIDS ARE FASTER,
SOME MIGHT BE SLOW,
OTHERS DON'T ALWAYS CATCH,
A FEW CAN'T REALLY THROW."

"WHEN YOU SAY MEAN THINGS,
EVEN THOUGH THEY TRIED,
YOU'LL MAKE OTHERS FEEL BAD,
THEY MIGHT JUST KEEP IT INSIDE."

"SOON WHAT WILL HAPPEN,
NO ONE WILL PLAY WITH YOU,

AND THEN WHAT DO YOU THINK,
YOU ARE GOING TO DO?"

MICHAEL REALLY UNDERSTOOD,
EVERYTHING HIS BROTHER SAID,
SO HE LET THE MESSAGES,
SINK INTO HIS HEAD.

FROM THAT DAY ON,
MICHAEL WAS A BETTER ATHLETE,
HE TRIED TO HELP OTHERS,
AS THEY WORKED TO COMPETE.

WHILE SOMETIMES HIS TEAM LOST,
SOMETIMES MICHAEL WON,
AND HE SOON REALIZED,
HE WAS HAVING MUCH MORE FUN.

EMMA IS DIFFERENT

EMMA WAS DIFFERENT,
KIND OF WEIRD THEY SAY,
SHE LIKED TO WEAR PAJAMAS,
IN THE MIDDLE OF THE DAY.

SHE DIDN'T USE AN UMBRELLA,
WHILE WALKING IN THE RAIN,
WHEN IT WAS TIME TO SLED,
SHE PULLED HER GREAT DANE.

WHEN MUSIC WAS PLAYING,
EMMA DANCED OFF BEAT,
AND SHE WALKED BACKWARDS,
WHEN IT WAS TIME TO TRICK OR TREAT.

SHE'D BEEN SEEN READING A BOOK,
FROM END TO START,
AND KIDS NOTICED HER HAIR,
HAD A REALLY CROOKED PART.

SHE MIGHT JUST WEAR ONE SOCK,
HER SHOES ON THE WRONG FEET,
AND WHEN EMMA POURED HER CEREAL,
SHE ADDED BROCCOLI AND A BEET.

YOU'D THINK BECAUSE SHE WAS DIFFERENT,
SHE'D SPEND ALL HER TIME ALONE,

AND NEVER HAVE A FRIEND,
CALL HER ON THE PHONE.

BUT EMMA WAS QUITE BUSY,
PEOPLE WANTED HER AROUND,
SHE WAS VERY WELL-LIKED,
BECAUSE SHE NEVER FROWNED.

EMMA NEVER HAD,
A MEAN WORD TO SAY,
WHEN IT WAS TIME FOR GAMES,
SHE LET EVERYBODY PLAY.

EMMA WAS HAPPY MOST OF THE TIME,
NO ONE EVER SAW HER POUT,
AND EVEN WHEN SHE GOT MAD,
SHE WAS NEVER KNOWN TO SHOUT.

EMMA SHARED HER TOYS,
SAID THANK YOU AND PLEASE,
AND EVEN SAID BLESS YOU,
WHEN SHE HEARD SOMEONE SNEEZE.

SO THOUGH EMMA WAS QUITE DIFFERENT,
AND KNEW IT FROM THE START,
SHE HAD A GREAT LIFE,
BECAUSE SHE HAD A HAPPY HEART.

EMMA WAS KIND TO PEOPLE,
AND ANIMALS, TOO,
AND I THINK SHE'D REALLY,
LIKE TO PLAY WITH YOU.

OUTSIDE

THERE ARE LOTS OF GOOD GAMES,
AND WAYS TO PLAY OUTSIDE,
YOU CAN COUNT TO TWENTY,
WHILE YOUR FRIENDS RUN AND HIDE.

OR GRAB A JUMP ROPE,
LET TWO PEOPLE TURN,
JUMPING AND RHYMING,
WITH PRACTICE YOU LEARN.

GRAB A PIECE OF CHALK,
MAKE 9 BOXES AND SKY BLUE,
IF YOU NEED HELP,
ASK YOUR PARENTS WHAT TO DO.

GET ON A BIKE,
PEDAL FAST AS YOU GO,
IF YOU'RE FIRST TO FINISH,
YOU'RE THE WINNER, YOU KNOW.

THERE'S A SIMPLE WAY TO WIN,
WHEN YOU PLAY TAG,
RUN FAST FROM WHO'S IT,
IF THEY ZIG YOU MUST ZAG.

OR YOU CAN PLAY FOOTBALL,
WITH TWO-HANDED TOUCH,
DON'T PLAY TACKLE,
IT'LL HURT TOO MUCH.

DOGS LOVE TO PLAY FETCH,
IN A FENCED YARD,
OR WALK WITH A LEASH,
IT'S NOT REALLY HARD.

GO TO A PARK,
PLAY WITH THE TOYS,
THEY REALLY ARE PUT THERE,
FOR BOTH GIRLS AND BOYS.

YOU CAN PLAY IN THE SUN,
OR IN THE SNOW,
OR AFTER THE RAIN,
LOOK FOR A RAINBOW.

IF YOU GO SOME PLACE,
TO CLIMB A ROCK WALL,

HOLD ON TIGHT,
SO YOU DON'T FALL.

MAKE UP A NEW GAME,
BY CHANGING AN OLD RULE,
THEN INVITE YOUR FRIENDS,
TO PLAY AFTER SCHOOL.

AND SOON YOU WILL SEE,
IF YOU GO OUT AND PLAY,
HOW MUCH FUN YOU CAN HAVE,
EACH AND EVERY DAY.

SEASONS

IN SOME PLACES,
WINTER IS COLD,
AND THE WIND,
IS VERY BOLD.

SOME ANIMALS HIBERNATE,
AND PLANTS AND TREES, TOO,
BECAUSE OF THEIR NATURE,
THEY KNOW WHAT TO DO.

THERE MIGHT BE LOTS OF SNOW,
OR EVEN SOME ICE,
AND PEOPLE FALL DOWN,
IT'S NOT VERY NICE.

BUT AFTER WINTER,
THERE SHOULD BE SPRING,
SOON THE BIRDS,
WILL START TO SING.

SPRING BRINGS RAIN,
INSTEAD OF SNOW,
AND GRASS AND FLOWERS AND TREES,
NEED RAIN TO GROW.

TEMPERATURES GET WARMER,
AND SO DOES THE SUN,
ICE WILL START BREAKING,
AND CREEKS START TO RUN.

WHEN SPRING TURNS TO SUMMER,
IT GETS REALLY HOT,
TRY TO DRINK EXTRA WATER,
IN CASE YOU FORGOT.

THE DAYS GET LONGER,
SCHOOL GETS OUT,
IF YOU HAVE SUMMER SCHOOL,
YOU WILL PROBABLY POUT.

IT SEEMS LIKE THERE'S LOTS,
OF SUMMER THINGS TO DO,
MORE KIDS WILL COME OUT,
AND PLAY WITH YOU.

BUT SUMMER WASN'T,
MEANT TO STAY,

SOON IT WILL BE,
LABOR DAY.

THAT'S THE UNOFFICIAL,
END OF SUMMER,
THE START OF SCHOOL,
CAN BE A BUMMER.

IN FALL THE SUN,
STAYS OUT LESS,
FIRST THE LEAVES CHANGE COLOR,
THEN THEY FALL AND MAKE A MESS.

YOU MIGHT STILL HAVE WARM DAYS,
BUT MORE OFTEN THAN NOT,
YOU'LL HAVE TO WEAR A COAT,
BECAUSE IT WON'T STAY HOT.

HALLOWEEN AND THANKSGIVING,
COME AND THEN,
BEFORE YOU KNOW IT,
IT'S WINTER AGAIN.

YOU MIGHT LIKE ONE BEST,
FOR SEVERAL DIFFERENT REASONS,
BUT THEY ALL SERVE THEIR PURPOSE,
AND WE NEED ALL FOUR SEASONS.

ME AND MY DOG

I LOVE MY DOG,
YES, I DO,
IF YOU MET HER,
YOU MIGHT, TOO.

WE HAVE FUN,
WALKING AROUND,
YOU CAN FIND US,
ALL OVER TOWN.

AND SOMETIMES WHEN,
WE'RE TAKING A WALK,
SHE SEES OTHER DOGS,
AND SHE TRIES TO TALK.

SHE REALLY LIKES,
WHEN I GIVE HER A TREAT,
SHE DOESN'T LIKE,
TO PLAY IN THE HEAT.

WE'LL GO TOGETHER,
AND TAKE A CAR RIDE,
SHE SITS IN THE FRONT SEAT,
RIGHT BY MY SIDE.

She looks out the front window,
She's really that tall,
And she'll go chase it,
When I throw a ball.

She sleeps with me,
When we go to bed,
And she'll fall asleep,
Right next to my head.

She's really happy,
When I give her a meal,
And I feed her right,
So she won't have to steal.

Most of the time,
She makes me smile,
She has her own,
Individual style.

I'VE TRAINED HER,
TO DO A FEW TRICKS,
BUT I CAN'T STOP HER,
FROM GIVING ME LICKS.

SHE SEEMS TO LISTEN,
WHEN I TALK TO HER,

AND SITS SO NICELY,
WHEN I BRUSH HER FUR.

I KNOW MY DOG,
IS MY FRIEND,
AND THIS STORY,
HAS COME TO AN END.

CAN YOU SPOT THE WRONG WORDS?

(FIND THE MISSPELLED WORDS)

IF THERE WAS A CHEER,
ON A STARE,
WOULD YOU SIT THERE?

IF U SAW A CAKE,
GO INTO A LAKE,
A PEACE WOULD YOU TAKE?

IF YOU TRIED TO DRINK,
AND THE WATER WAS PINK,
WOOD YOU POUR IT IN THE SINK?

IF YOU PICKED UP UR HAT,
AND OUT FLU A BAT,
WOULD DAT END THAT?

IF THE GRASS WAS BLEW,
AND GOT ON YOUR SHOE,
WHAT WOULD YOU DEW?

IF YOU'RE HARE FELL OUT,
AND YOU GREW A SNOUT,
MITE YOU SHOUT?

IF U SAW A CAR,
N IT LOOKED LIKE A STAR,
WOULD IT GO FAR?

IF NITE,
WAS ALWAYS LITE,
WOULD IT BEE A FRIGHT?

COULD A FROGG,
THAT LOOKS LIKE A DOG,
LIVE INN A LOG?

IF U COULD SPELL,
ALL YORE WORDS WELL,
COULD THE TEACHER TELL?

SINCE THIS IS THE END,
CAN U SEND,
YOUR BOOK TWO A FRIEND?

TALENTS

LOTS OF KIDS LIKE JUDY,
BECAUSE SHE LIKES TO SHARE,
PATTY HAS LOTS OF FRIENDS,
BY KNOWING HOW TO CARE.

DENNIS IS POPULAR,
HE'S PRETTY GOOD AT SPORTS.
AND MICHELE'S ALWAYS HAPPY,
AND NEVER OUT OF SORTS.

HIS FRIENDS LIKE EDDIE,
HE ALWAYS WANTS TO PLAY,
OTHERS LIKE JOHN,
HE KNOWS JUST WHAT TO SAY.

MARY IS A GOOD READER,
KATHLEEN CAN DO MATH REALLY FAST,
DANA'S GOOD AT HISTORY,
LOVES LEARNING ABOUT THE PAST.

JILL IS ONE OF THOSE,
WHO'S CREATIVE WITH HER HAIR,
AND WHEN DENNY PLAYS GAMES,
HE ALWAYS PLAYS FAIR.

MIKE IS REALLY GOOD,
AT COLORING BETWEEN THE LINES,
AMY'S BROTHER'S DEAF,
SO SHE LEARNED HOW TO SIGN.

MEGAN IS PRETTY GOOD,
AT DOING HOMEWORK FIRST,
ADRIAN WILL PLAY WITH ANYONE,
EVEN AT THEIR WORST.

COLIN IS GOOD AT HELPING,
OTHERS CROSS THE STREET,
AND DARREN JUST LIKES TO SMILE,
AT EVERYONE HE MEETS.

ERIN IS ALWAYS FIRST,
AT FINISHING HER CHORES,
AND DIANE STAYS IN THE GAME,
BY ALWAYS KEEPING SCORES.

MELANIE HAS TO WAIT,
TO KNOW WHAT SHE DOES BEST,
BUT EVERYONE HAS SOMETHING,
THEY DO BETTER THAN THE REST.

THE LESSON TO BE LEARNED,
JUST BETWEEN US TWO,
LOOK FOR THE GOOD IN OTHERS,
THEY WILL LOOK FOR IT IN YOU.

RANDOM COUNTING RHYMES

ONE TWO,
KICK YOUR SHOE,
THREE FOUR,
SPIN ON THE FLOOR.

FIVE SIX,
DOGGIE LICKS,
SEVEN EIGHT,
NEVER HATE.

NINE TEN,
START AGAIN.
TEN NINE,
TOUCH A STOP SIGN.

EIGHT SEVEN,
TWELVE ELEVEN.
SIX FIVE,
A BUSY BEEHIVE,

TOUCH YOUR KNEE.
TWO ONE,
START AGAIN

SIX EIGHT,
STAY UP LATE,
TWELVE TEN,
START AGAIN.

ONE THREE,
LOVE IS THE KEY,
FIVE SEVEN,
LOOK TO HEAVEN.

NINE IS FINE,
TEN STARTS AGAIN,
NUMBERS CAN BE FUN,
IF YOU COUNT FROM ONE.

www.ingramcontent.com/pod-product-compliance
Lightning Source LLC
LaVergne TN
LVHW070217080526
838202LV00067B/6837